T4-ADP-130
LIBRARY SYSTEM

**3650 Summit Boulevard
West Palm Beach, FL 33406**

FUSION

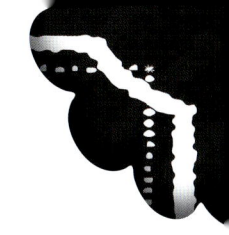

Deconstructed Diets

BREAK DOWN A BENTO BOX

by Shalini Vallepur

BEARPORT PUBLISHING

Minneapolis, Minnesota

Library of Congress Cataloging-in-Publication Data is available at www.loc.gov or upon request from the publisher.

ISBN: 978-1-64747-522-2 (hardcover)
ISBN: 978-1-64747-529-1 (paperback)
ISBN: 978-1-64747-536-9 (ebook)

© 2021 Booklife Publishing

This edition is published by arrangement with Booklife Publishing.

North American adaptations © 2021 Bearport Publishing Company. All rights reserved. No part of this publication may be reproduced in whole or in part, stored in any retrieval system, or transmitted in any form or by any means, electronic, mechanical, photocopying, recording, or otherwise, without written permission from the publisher.

For more information, write to Bearport Publishing, 5357 Penn Avenue South, Minneapolis, MN 55419. Printed in the United States of America.

PHOTO CREDITS

All images are courtesy of Shutterstock.com, unless otherwise specified. With thanks to Getty Images, Thinkstock Photo, and iStockphoto. Front Cover & Recurring Images - Akane1988, HappyPicture, kolopach, Nataly Studio, uiliaaa, Vectorpocket, Yamori Oomori, VWORLD, Tortuga. 4-5 - ilkayalptekin, istetiana, Monkey Business Images, Morphart Creation, Zonda, Reamolko, mamormo, OlgaChernyak, Ansty. 6-7 - Chika.S, icosha, norikko. 8-9 - Breaking The Wall, Larisa Blinova - Olga Danylenko. 10-11 - Alphonsine Sabine, bonchan, Dernkadel, Hennadii H. 12-13 - bonchan, Axel Wolf, Gray Cat, Iriska48, kisasage, li hanna, mything, Spreadthesign, Yamori Oomori, nada54. 14-15 - Abscent, Akane1988, Anna.zabella, kazoka, Pixel-Shot, thaweerat, Maquiladora. 16-17 - anarociogf, BlueRingMedia, HappyPictures, Jakinnboaz, Again Peace. 18-19 - Magdanatka, Pixel-Shot, Somchai Som. 20-21 - Galliina, MShima, yajima. 22-23 - Anna Klepper, CloudyStock, Mali Jasmine, Nataliya Arzamasova, SewCream, Anna.zabella.

CONTENTS

What Is a Diet? 4

Beautiful Bento 6

Break Down a Bento 8

Rice 10

Vegetables 12

Meat 14

Tamagoyaki 16

Smart Swaps 18

Bento Box Fun 20

Bento around the World 22

Glossary 24

Index 24

WHAT IS A DIET?

Your diet is what you eat and drink in a day. The foods we eat help us to grow and be healthy.

Our meals are made from lots of different **ingredients**. It can be hard to know exactly what is in our food or where it comes from.

Burritos are made from many different ingredients.

Let's look at all the ingredients in a bento box!

BEAUTIFUL BENTO

Bento comes from Japan. It is usually one meal packed into a box. Bento boxes have been eaten by people in Japan for hundreds of years.

Bento boxes can be eaten at any time of day.

There are many types of bento boxes. Some can be bought in stores, and others are made at home.

On sale in a store

At a picnic

BREAK DOWN A BENTO

A bento box can have all kinds of food.

Bento boxes usually have rice or noodles.

Rice

Vegetables

The box can be split into different parts.

8

Bento box

Tamagoyaki

Tonkatsu

DID YOU KNOW?

The box can be made of many things, such as wood or plastic.

Let's learn about the ingredients.

RICE

Rice is usually part of a bento box. Japanese rice gets sticky when it is cooked.

Uncooked rice

Cooked rice

Rice balls

The rice is sticky enough to be made into different shapes. **Onigiri** are rice balls.

Rice has a lot of things that are good for our bodies.

Plum

A **pickled** plum on rice looks like the Japanese flag.

11

VEGETABLES

Most bento boxes include vegetables. These vegetables are sometimes pickled.

Cabbage ···> Cut cabbage + Rice vinegar = Pickled cabbage

Carrot ···> Shredded carrot + Rice vinegar = Pickled carrot

Rice vinegar pickles the vegetables and gives them flavor.

Cucumber   Sliced cucumber   Rice vinegar   =   Pickled cucumber

Pickled vegetables are still crunchy.

Radishes are crunchy, too. Lots of different vegetables can be found in a bento box.

Radish

MEAT

Tonkatsu is made from pig meat.

Pig → Pork + Breadcrumbs = Tonkatsu

Pork is mixed with breadcrumbs to make tonkatsu.

Pig meat is called pork.

14

Tonkatsu is tasty, but it can be unhealthy because it is fried. Foods that are fried often have fat that is bad for our bodies.

Fried in oil

Baked in an oven

Tonkatsu can be baked in an oven to make it more healthy.

TAMAGOYAKI

Tamagoyaki is made from eggs that are rolled up. It can be cut into small pieces and put in a bento box.

Eggs

+

Soy sauce

=

Tamagoyaki

The eggs are usually mixed with other ingredients. Then, they are cooked in a square pan and rolled.

Eggs have many **nutrients** to make you strong and healthy.

Tamagoyaki can be filled with vegetables, too.

SMART SWAPS

The ingredients in a bento box can fit different diets.

SUITABLE FOR VEGETARIANS

Swap meat for **tofu** to make a bento for a **vegetarian**.

Tofu

Try swapping white rice for brown rice. Brown rice is better for you than white rice.

Brown rice

White rice

BENTO BOX FUN

A **kyaraben** is a fun type of bento. The food inside the box is made to look like different animals and shapes.

Which is your favorite?

BENTO AROUND THE WORLD

Bento boxes can be found all around the world.

22

Will you have sandwiches or spaghetti?

You can put whatever you want in a bento box!

23

GLOSSARY

ingredients — the different foods that are used to make something

kyaraben — a style of making bento box foods look like animals or other special shapes

nutrients — things that humans need to grow and stay healthy

onigiri — food made from rice that is often shaped into triangles

pickled — put in vinegar to make food last longer

tamagoyaki — a Japanese egg dish made of thin cooked egg that has been rolled

tonkatsu — food made of pig meat that has been coated with breadcrumbs and then fried or baked

vegetarian — a person who does not eat meat

INDEX

eggs 16–17
Japan 6, 10–11
pickled 11–13
pork 14
rice 8, 10–11, 19
tofu 18
tonkatsu 9, 14–15
vegetables 8, 12–13, 17
vinegar 12–13